Crawlers

DAVID ORME

Rans♦m

Crawlers
by David Orme
Illustrated by Jorge Mongiovi and Ulises Carpintero
Cover photograph: © Erkki Makkonen

Published by Ransom Publishing Ltd.
Radley House, 8 St. Cross Road, Winchester, Hampshire SO23 9HX, UK
www.ransom.co.uk

ISBN   978 184167 464 3

First published in 2011

Printed in India by Imprint Digital Ltd.
Originally published in 1998 by Stanley Thornes Publishers Ltd.

A CIP catalogue record of this book is available from the British Library.

CONTENTS

NOT FOR THE PUBLIC TO KNOW
TOP SECRET
ZONE 13 FILES ONLY

4

THE MUMMY

The big metal box rested on a table in the middle of the laboratory. The scientists stood next to it. A group of important-looking visitors stood nearby.

'Welcome to the Energy Research Laboratories, ladies and gentlemen. I am Dr Talbot. I am a scientist researching energy waves. As you know, Dr Williams here is an archaeologist. The third person you will meet is in that box there.'

The visitors laughed. They knew that the
visitor in the box had been dead for centuries.

Dr Williams had brought a mummy from
the museum where she worked. She hoped
that Dr Talbot's new invention would tell her
a lot about it.

'The high-energy particles I have discovered
can be used to let us see deep inside objects,
even solid rock or metal. It is too powerful to

use on living things. It can damage their cells. That won't worry the person in the box!'

'Why can't you just cut the mummy open?' asked one of the visitors.

'That would destroy it,' said Dr Williams. 'This way the mummy is undamaged.'

Dr Talbot switched on the machine. On a large screen, the visitors could see colour pictures of a slice through the mummy.

'What are those tiny round things there?' asked a visitor.

'They are probably parasite eggs,' said Dr Williams. 'Some sort of insect. We find all sorts of things inside mummies.'

ooo//ooo

The visitors and scientists had gone home. The laboratory was in darkness. Inside the scanner, the wrappings on the mummy were moving. It was as if something inside was trying to get out. A hole appeared, and then another. A brown maggot wriggled along the wrappings, then dropped onto the floor of the box.

Soon hundreds of them were crawling across the laboratory floor, looking for dark, warm places to hide ...

NOT FOR THE PUBLIC TO KNOW
TOP SECRET
ZONE 13 FILES ONLY

2

DEATH IN THE LIFT

Late that night, two security men were patrolling the building. They took the lift to the second floor. Dr Talbot's laboratory was there.

The lift suddenly stopped and the lights went out. Within seconds, an emergency light flickered on.

'Power cut,' said one of the guards. 'The back-up generator should come on in a minute.'

But nothing happened. The other guard, a big Scotsman known as Jock, used his radio.

'Hey, Ted! Harry and I are stuck in the lift. The emergency generator hasn't cut in. Can you check it out, mate?'

Ted's voice crackled.

'I'm already on my way, Jock.'

The two men sat on the floor of the lift and waited. At last, they heard Ted's voice.

'I'm in the power room. Nothing is working here. I've only got my torch. I'm opening the switch cupboard now.'

A terrible scream came from the radio. Jock and Harry jumped up in alarm.

'Ted! What's happened? What's wrong, mate?'

The screams went on. At last they died away and stopped. The two men looked at each other.

'Ted must have touched a live wire, or something.'

Harry shook his head.

'It would have been quick if he had done that. That screaming went on and on.'

He suddenly remembered something.

'That mummy they brought in. Mummies have – curses!'

'Don't be a fool!' muttered Jock. 'That thing's been dead for thousands of years!'

Just then two things happened. First, the emergency light flickered and went out.

The second thing started as a faint scraping sound. It seemed to come from the wooden floor of the lift. It got louder and louder. The men could see nothing in the darkness, but they could feel something – something that tickled – crawling over their feet ...

NOT FOR THE PUBLIC TO KNOW

TOP SECRET

ZONE 13 FILES ONLY

16

IN THE LABORATORY

When Dr Talbot arrived in the morning, he saw police cars and ambulances outside the building. The director was waiting for him. He looked very pale.

'What's happened?'

'The security guards are dead! Their bodies are in a terrible state. The police are searching the building. Can you go to your laboratory? I don't want them opening anything that could be harmful.'

The power was still off, so Dr Talbot rushed up the stairs. Two policemen were waiting for him. Dr Talbot unlocked the door.

'Come in. The power isn't on, so you can't harm anything.'

The laboratory had a strange, musty smell. The high-energy scanner with the mummy inside was still in the centre of the room.

'What's that?'

'It's a mummy! I've been doing an experiment with Dr Williams from the museum.'

The policeman looked in the box.

'Phew! What a stink! This mummy looks in a bad way!'

Dr Talbot looked in the box. The last time he had seen the mummy, it was in good condition. Now it was full of round, ragged holes. A rotting smell came from it.

'I don't understand it! Yesterday, it was perfect! I'm not an archaeologist, of course,

but I know something odd is going on. Dr
Williams will be furious! Her precious
mummy, full of holes!'

'Yes,' said one of the policemen. 'Just like the security guards.'

THE INSECT EXPERT

When Dr Williams arrived from the museum, she brought someone with her. Mike Roberts worked at the same museum. He was an entomologist, an expert on insects.

'When you described the holes, I knew it had to be insects,' said Dr Williams. 'Do you remember those parasite eggs we saw on the scan?'

'But those eggs have been dead for centuries!' said Dr Talbot.

Mike Roberts peered closely at the mummy. 'Maybe not,' he said. 'Now what have we here?'

He took a pair of tweezers out of a small case and fished inside one of the holes. He pulled out a fat, brown maggot.

'This one's dead, anyway,' he said. 'Not all of them managed to tunnel their way out.'

'Do you know what it is?'

'I've never seen anything like it before. Tell me, Dr Talbot. What effect do your energy particles have on living things?'

'We would never use them on living things. It damages their cells.'

'And damaged cells lead to mutations! Dr Talbot, I think you have woken up something very nasty here. Parasites so deadly they can tunnel straight into living flesh.'

'But where are they now? There's no sign of them!'

'They may have changed by now. Each maggot may have turned into a chrysalis. Something even more deadly may come out of those.'

He put the dead maggot into a small bottle. 'I'll have a good look at this.'

ooo//ooo

Dr Talbot couldn't do any work at the laboratory. The mummy was put into a sealed box and taken away. He walked out of the building with Dr Williams and the entomologist.

As they were shaking hands, they heard a shout. They turned back to the building. It looked as if black smoke was pouring from the top of it.

'A fire!'

That's not a fire,' said Dr Roberts. 'That's them! They've hatched – and they can fly!'

IN THE EMPTY HOUSE

A mile from the laboratory was a row of empty houses. They would soon be knocked down. The doors and windows had been boarded up, but homeless people had broken in. They used the houses as a place to sleep.

Ben was living in one of the houses. He had run away from a foster home. He had had a really bad time there. He would rather live in a dirty old house by himself than be with people he hated.

That morning he slept late, even though it wasn't very comfortable sleeping on the floor.

Usually the daylight shone through the cracks in the window boards and woke him. Today it was still dark. He heard strange rustling and whirring sounds.

Ben kept a box of matches and a candle nearby, in case something happened in the night.

He reached for it and lit his candle. He looked around the room.

Now he knew what the noise was, and why it was still dark.

Every inch of the room was covered with crawling black insects! They covered the windows and doors, and hung in great clumps from the ceiling. The rustling noise came from their hard wing cases scraping against each other.

Some of the insects were flying round the room, bumping into the walls. Some were crawling over Ben's sleeping bag.

Ben leapt to his feet with a yell. He rushed to the door, then stopped because it was covered in insects. He grabbed at the door handle. That was covered in them, too. He felt them crunch and go wet in his hands as he pulled the door open. He rushed down the stairs and pushed his way into the street.

Luckily he always slept in his clothes! Ben was shaking with horror. There was a small café nearby. He just had enough money for a cup of tea. It was hard to drink the tea, as his hands were shaking.

A TV was on in the corner of the café. A reporter was speaking.

'Mike Roberts, from the city museum, said that the insects could be deadly. No one knows where they are now.'

Ben stared at the TV. He knew! The museum was in the town centre. Not far. He gulped down his tea and set off.

6

'YOU'LL BE EATEN ALIVE!'

Mike Roberts was looking at Ben's clothes through a magnifying glass.

'Eggs! They're all over you! They must have crawled over you when you were asleep! Come on, quickly. There's a shower here in the museum. Give me your clothes and I'll burn them. Have a shower, as hot as you can. Use this insecticide.'

'But what am I going to wear?'

'I'll find you something. Hurry up, before those eggs hatch. You'll be eaten alive!'

Ben scrubbed himself under the hot shower. The insects must have got right inside his clothes. He could see the small brown eggs dropping from his body and disappearing down the drain at the bottom of the shower.

Mike had found some clothes.

'Right. Get these on. Then show me that
house of yours.'

Ben stayed in the car while Mike went into
the house. He was dressed from head to foot
in protective clothing. He carried a large tank
of powerful insecticide.

Mike went up the stairs. He had guessed that the insects were harmless at this stage. They would lay their eggs on a living creature, then die. The eggs would hatch into maggots, which would burrow into living flesh to feed. That was when they were dangerous.

Mike pushed into the room. It was still crammed with insects. He started spraying. To his alarm, the insecticide seemed to have no effect!

Mike did not know that someone else had lived in the old house. In a downstairs room, a tramp had been sleeping. The tramp was dead, but his body moved as if it were still alive.

Now, the brown maggots sensed that fresh meat was near.

Upstairs.

NOT FOR THE PUBLIC TO KNOW
TOP SECRET
ZONE 13 FILES ONLY

FIRE !

Mike Roberts stopped spraying. This was hopeless! All he was doing was annoying the insects. They flew round his head, trying to find a way in through his protective clothing.

He opened the door and started down the stairs. With a shock he saw the brown maggots below. They could bore through solid wood. His suit wasn't going to protect him.

He rushed back into the room and shut the door. Useless. They could eat their way in.

Out of the corner of his eye he saw something flicker. Ben had left his candle alight. The flying insects had knocked it over. Some old newspaper had caught alight.

Then he saw that the insects on the paper were bursting into flame. They burnt instantly!

Grabbing the paper, Mike pushed it against the wall. It burst into a sheet of flame.

He could kill the insects, but how could he get out? The fire was spreading round the room. Outside, the flesh-hungry maggots had already reached the door.

In despair, Mike dived at the window. He would rather fall to his death than be burnt or eaten alive.

To his amazement, he only fell a short way. There was a flat roof just under the window! He scrambled to the edge and found a drainpipe. He slid to the ground.

Ben was relieved when the insect scientist appeared. The flames had taken hold of the whole building by now.

'Well, that's one way of doing it,' said Mike.
'I think I've got the lot. Let's head back. I need
a shower now!'

They headed back to the museum.

In the drain, under the shower, the hungry brown maggots were waiting.

ABOUT THE AUTHOR

David Orme is an expert on strange, unexplained events. For his protection (and yours) we cannot show a photograph of him.

David created the Zone 13 files to record the cases he studied. Some of these files really do involve aliens, but many do not. Aliens are not everywhere. Just in most places.

These stories are all taken from the Zone 13 files. They will not be here for long. Read them while you can.

But don't close your eyes when you go to sleep at night. **They** will be watching you.